For my sister, Angela, and my friends at Hurlingham School
- I.H.

For Jude, Ellie, and Dana, who sprinkle stars
onto bedtime stories
- A.G.

tiger tales

5 River Road, Suite 128, Wilton, CT 06097
Published in the United States 2018
Originally published in Great Britain 2017 by Little Tiger Press
Text copyright © 2017 Isabel Harris
Illustrations copyright © 2017 Ada Grey
ISBN-13: 978-1-68010-078-5
ISBN-10: 1-68010-078-5
Printed in China
LTP/1400/1985/0817
10 9 8 7 6 5 4 3 2 1

For more insight and activities, visit us at www.tigertalesbooks.com

THE MOON MAN

by Isabel Harris   Illustrated by Ada Grey

tiger tales

In the sunny corner of a wheat field grew
a great oak tree. Sitting under its branches were
Cat, Rabbit, and Squirrel.

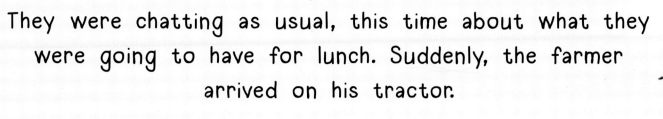

They were chatting as usual, this time about what they were going to have for lunch. Suddenly, the farmer arrived on his tractor.

He put up a scarecrow in the middle of the field and then drove away.

Of course, you know what a scarecrow is,
but Cat and Squirrel didn't, so they asked wise old Rabbit.

"It's a crow scarer! I'm sure!" Rabbit said,
hopping up to take a closer look.
"He smells like buttercups and fresh grass," sniffed Cat.
"And he has a friendly face," smiled Squirrel.

For the rest of the day, the friends played happily beside the scarecrow. And when the sun began to set, they went to sleep, just like always, in their comfy homes.

There was a full moon that night and
in the moonlight, Fox, Owl, and Hedgehog
spotted a strange new thing in the field.
"What is it?" squeaked Hedgehog.
"I think it's a man," said Fox.
"From the moon!" hooted Owl.
"A Moon Man! Is he dangerous?"
cried Hedgehog.

Owl shook his head. "I don't think so," he said.
"He must be hungry," added Fox. "He's traveled a long way."
So the friends decided to make a feast for the Moon Man.

All night, they gathered tasty treats and put them at his feet.
Then, yawning, they headed home to bed.

When the sun came up, Cat, Rabbit,
and Squirrel met at the great oak tree.

"Wow!" Squirrel gasped.
"He gave us food!" purred Cat. "Thank you, Crow Scarer!"
"Let's eat!" said Rabbit, hopping around happily.

"We must give him a thank-you present,"
smiled Cat when all the food was gone.
So for the rest of the day, the friends picked beautiful
flowers and decorated the scarecrow with them.

"Night night, Crow Scarer,"
yawned Squirrel as
afternoon turned to dusk.
"Sweet dreams."

When it was dark out, Fox, Owl, and Hedgehog
returned to find that the feast had disappeared
and the Moon Man was covered in flowers.

"He ate it all!" cheered Fox happily.
"And he picked those flowers
to take home," said Hedgehog.
"Yes," nodded Owl wisely,
"because there are no flowers
on the moon."

"Do you think he's homesick?" wondered Hedgehog.
"I would be," agreed Fox. "But how can he get home?"
"Let's build him a rocket!" they all shouted together.

So Owl drew a plan, while Fox and
Hedgehog gathered materials.

The friends worked hard, and soon the rocket was almost ready.
Hedgehog and Fox tied the final twig in place.
"Perfect!" hooted Owl as he poured honey
inside for fuel.

Then, before the friends headed home,
Owl tucked some of his old feathers inside
the Moon Man's sleeves to help him fly.

Early the next morning, the farmer arrived at the field. He was puzzled to find the scarecrow covered in flowers and feathers. So he cleaned them off and moved the scarecrow to a faraway field.

Cat, Rabbit, and Squirrel watched the farmer sadly.
"Thanks for the food, magic Crow Scarer," said Cat.
"I will miss him," sniffed Squirrel.

That night, Fox, Owl, and Hedgehog
were happy to see that the Moon Man
had flown away in his rocket.

They looked up and saw a star shooting across the dark sky.
"There he goes!" the animals cheered as they imagined their
friend back on the moon with his family.
"Good-bye, Moon Man!" whispered Hedgehog.
"And good night."